Arlene Alda's

ABC

6/99

Nicholas —
hope you enjoy
this way cool alphabet
book! Happy Birthday!
We love you & miss you
Love,
Kathryn & Joel

Tricycle Press
Berkeley, California

Thank you, Jay

🚲

Tricycle Press
P.O. Box 7123
Berkeley, California 94707

Book design by Tasha Hall

Library of Congress Cataloging-in-Publication Data

Alda, Arlene, 1933—
[ABC]
Arlene Alda's ABC.
p.   cm.
Originally published: Millbrae, Calif. : Celestial Arts, c1981.
Summary: A collection of photographs of things in our environment
that resemble the letters of the alphabet.
ISBN 1-883672-01-5
1. English language--Alphabet--Juvenile literature.
[1. Alphabet.]   I. Title.   II. Title: ABC.
PE1155.A45 1993
[E]--dc20   93-24999
                                               CIP
                                                AC

First published by Celestial Arts, 1981.
First Tricycle Press printing, 1993.

Manufactured in Hong Kong

3 4 5 6 — 01 00 99 98 97

Years ago, when I first started taking pictures, I took hundreds of shots of people, animals, landscapes, seascapes, and objects. Everything was of interest to me, without a sense of artistic discrimination.

As I got better at what I did, and as my eye became more discerning, I began to realize that my enthusiasm was being enhanced by developing a selective and expressive eye with my camera. It was with this spirit of selectivity that I began wandering and taking photos of things in our environment that resembled alphabet letters. It was a visual game for me. Ironically, my game-playing and selectivity led me back to a time when I was much less sophisticated.

As a child, I remember looking up at the sky and noticing the clouds as they changed shape and forms. I played the game of imagining faces in those white and grey puffs. Rocks were another rich source of imagined faces, as were water and sand. How wonderful it was to recapture the excitement of those early "discoveries," by looking around with a fresh vision.

To see—as a child. That's what this book is all about.

Arlene Alda

The world is rich in shapes,
textures, designs, and colors.

This book is a visual poem.
It speaks of the ordinary
in a transformed way.

If you look around you,
you might even see...

THE ALPHABET

A

B

cCCc

D

E

F

G

G

G

G

H

I

K

L

M

P

Q

R

·U·

VVVV

W

X

Y

Z